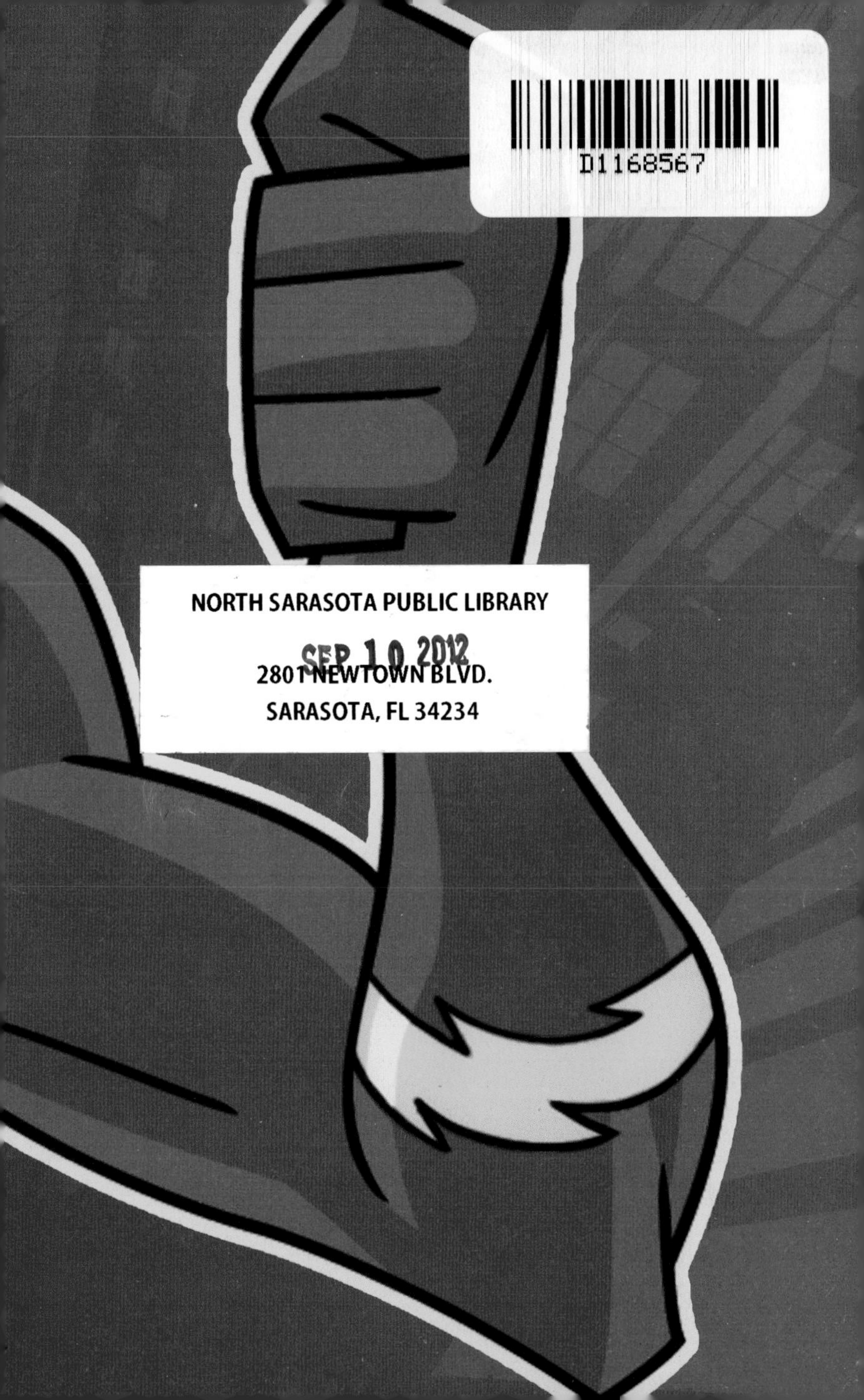

AFTER BEING STRUCK BY A BOLT OF LIGHTNING AND
DOUSED WITH CHEMICALS, POLICE SCIENTIST BARRY
ALLEN BECAME THE FASTEST MAN ON EARTH . . .

SUPER DC HEROES

THE FLASH

WRITTEN BY
SEAN TULIEN

ILLUSTRATED BY
DAN SCHOENING,
MIKE DeCARLO, AND
LEE LOUGHRIDGE

CLOCK KING'S TIME BOMB

STONE ARCH BOOKS
a capstone imprint

Published by Stone Arch Books in 2012
A Capstone Imprint
151 Good Counsel Drive, P.O. Box 669
Mankato, Minnesota 56002
www.capstonepub.com

STAR25059

Library of Congress Cataloging-in-Publication Data
Tulien, Sean.
  Clock King's time bomb / written by Sean Tulien ; illustrated by Dan
Schoening.
     p. cm. -- (DC super heroes)
  ISBN-13: 978-1-4342-2626-6 (library binding)
  ISBN-13: 978-1-4342-3412-4 (pbk.)
  1. Flash (Fictitious character)--Juvenile fiction. 2. Superheroes--Juvenile
fiction. 3. Supervillains--Juvenile fiction. 4. Time--Juvenile fiction. 5. Clocks
and watches--Juvenile fiction. [1. Superheroes--Fiction. 2. Supervillains--
Fiction. 3. Time--Fiction. 4. Clocks and watches--Fiction.] I. Schoening, Dan,
ill. II. Title.
  PZ7.T822964Cl 2012
  813.6--dc22   2011006697

Summary: New Zealanders are about to ring in the New Year. But when the
clock strikes midnight . . . it stops! Technology malfunctions throughout the
entire time zone. Then the Clock King appears, spouting his evil plan. When
the clock strikes midnight across all time zones, the world will be doomed! The
Flash must find the location of the Time Bomb or the whole planet will fall
under Clock King's command.

Art Director: Bob Lentz
Designer: Brann Garvey
Production Specialist: Michelle Biedscheid

Printed in the United States of America in Stevens Point, Wisconsin.
032011
006111WZF11

TABLE OF CONTENTS

CHAPTER 1

MIDNIGHT MADNESS. 4

CHAPTER 2

MORE BAD NEWS 15

CHAPTER 3

RUNAWAY TRAIN. 24

CHAPTER 4

TIME TRAP. 30

CHAPTER 5

TURBULENCE. 37

MIDNIGHT MADNESS

Barry Allen sat in his lab at the Central City police station early in the morning of New Year's Eve. He examined evidence from a recent crime scene. Behind him, his TV was set to a worldwide news channel.

Like many people, Barry tried to stay informed about current events. However, unlike others, Barry had a special reason. He was secretly the super-speedy super hero known as the Flash! By keeping his eye out for bad news, Flash would know when his help would be needed most.

Suddenly, a news flash caught his attention. "This just in from Auckland, New Zealand," the TV newscaster reported. "Technology throughout the entire time zone has begun to malfunction!"

Barry grew concerned. "At the stroke of New Zealand's new year, a strange electronic interference damaged all digital timers and clocks," reported the newscaster. "As a result, cell doors suddenly opened at midnight at Auckland Prison, releasing all of the prison's inmates."

Barry frowned. *This is bad news,* he thought.

"Unfortunately," the reporter added, "we can't show you any footage of the event. All video cameras in the area have stopped working as well. But rest assured, we will keep our viewers updated as —" CRACKLE!

Suddenly, strange, impossible clock times flashed across the screen — 17:83 p.m., 37:42 a.m., and countless others. Then, an oval shape began to form in the swirling mass of pixilated digits. A moment later, a face emerged from the numbers — one with a bowler hat, clock-face glasses, and an evil grin.

Barry gasped. "It's the Clock King!"

"Good morning, people of Earth," the super-villain said into the camera. "And, since I'm broadcasting worldwide — good afternoon and good evening!"

The villain leaned back in his chair. "I hate to interrupt the news, but they weren't telling you the whole story," Clock King mocked. He patted his hand on a strange-looking device next to him.

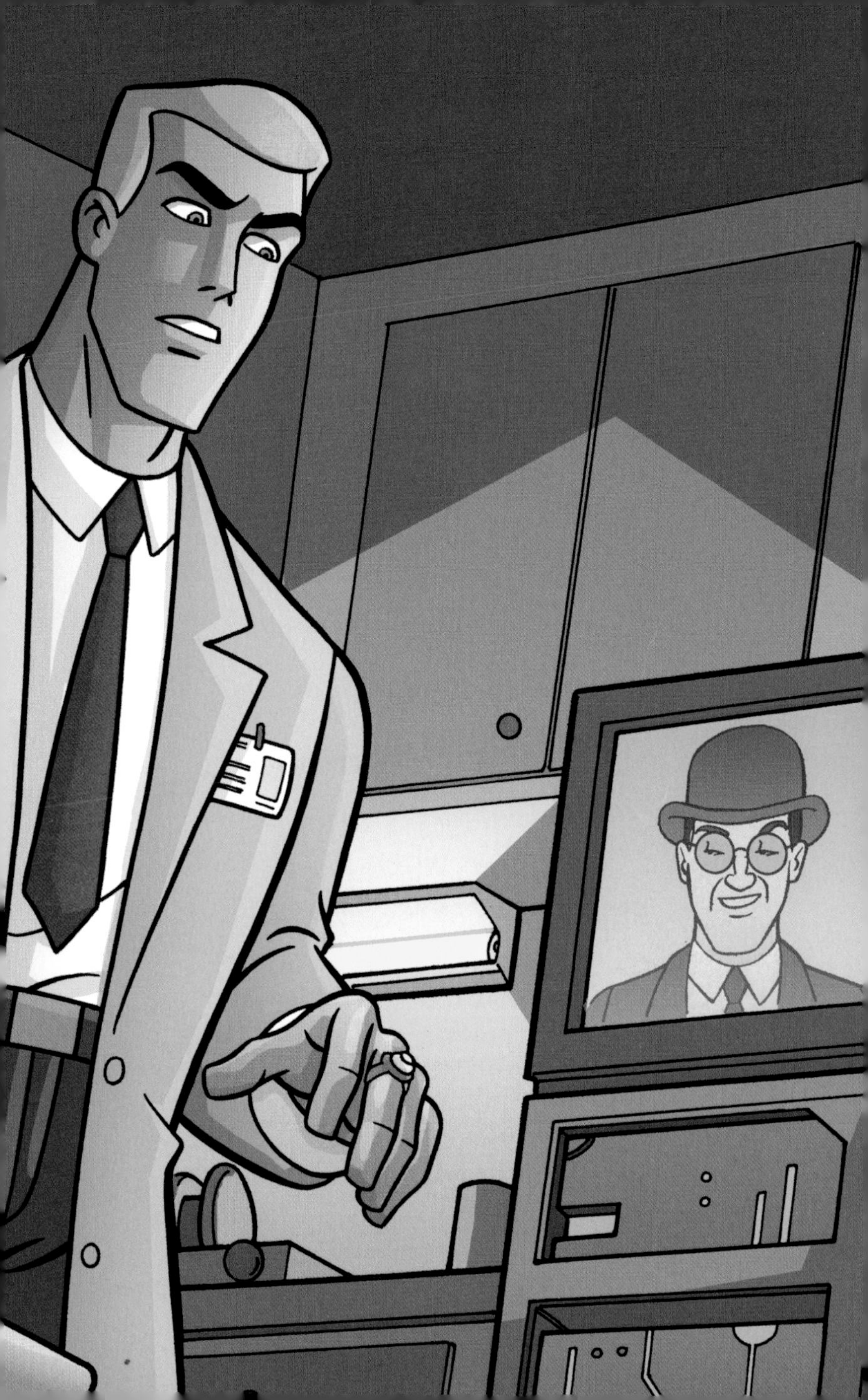

Various clock faces jutted outward from the object's base. It looked like it came from a science-fiction movie.

"You see, New Zealand's prison riot is just the beginning," the villain warned. "Using my Time Bomb, I will stop all clocks across the entire globe, time zone by time zone. In less than 24 hours, all digital clocks will break, and every piece of technology that depends on clocks will malfunction. All computers, all forms of transportation, everything dependent on time, will be useless when the clock strikes midnight in the final time zone!"

The villain beamed with pride. "Welcome to the YCK — the year of the Clock King!" he shouted. The villain quickly composed himself, and added, "Oh, and please have a safe and happy New Year."

BZZZT! The TV went blank. Suddenly, Barry heard his fellow police officers outside the lab scramble around. Undoubtedly, they were working to help out however they could.

And so was Barry, but not as a police officer. He left the lab and calmly walked toward the stairway. *ZOOOM!*

Faster than the eye could see, Barry donned his Flash costume and dashed outside. He ran westward across the United States and the Pacific Ocean, skipping over the water. At super-speed, Flash would reach Auckland, New Zealand in no time.

Flash came to a sudden stop inside the metal doors of the Auckland Prison. As he looked over the countless jail cells, he saw that they were empty. All the prisoners were fighting with the guards!

Flash grabbed a megaphone off a nearby wall. "THIS IS THE FLASH SPEAKING," his voice echoed loudly within the concrete walls of the prison.

Every prisoner and guard stopped fighting. They turned to look at the Flash. The super hero was amused by the blank faces that stared back. He could tell that at least some of them recognized him.

Flash spoke into the megaphone again. "WOULD YOU INMATES KINDLY RETURN TO YOUR CELLS, PLEASE?" he said.

Half the criminals immediately ran to their cells and closed the gates. However, the other half of the prisoners stayed right where they were. One of them shook his balled-up fist. "Why should we listen to some guy wearing red and gold pajamas?" he challenged.

The prisoners laughed at the joke. Flash tensed his leg muscles. "If you're smart," Flash warned, "you'll do as you're told."

The burly man let out a belly-laugh. "There's only one of you," he pointed out. "And there are hundreds of us!"

"You can count!" Flash joked. "I'm quite impressed."

Some of the prisoners laughed. This made the burly prisoner angry. He raised his fist and prepared to punch a nearby security guard.

 Flash disappeared.

A second later, the loudmouthed prisoner went sliding across the floor. **WHAM!** He slammed into a wall inside of a cell. **CLANK!** The cell door slammed shut behind him.

"Anyone else feeling smart?" Flash said, reappearing in the center of the remaining criminals.

"GET HIM!" one convict yelled. They all ran toward the Flash, surrounding him in a circle.

ZWWWHOOOMMMM! At superspeed, Flash traveled behind each man and gave him a slight push.

THUD! All at once, the prisoners fell forward and crashed into each other. They fell to the ground in a heap. All of them were unconscious — but none were seriously injured.

The warden walked up to the Flash and shook his hand. "Thanks so much, Flash!" he said. "Things were really getting out of control here."

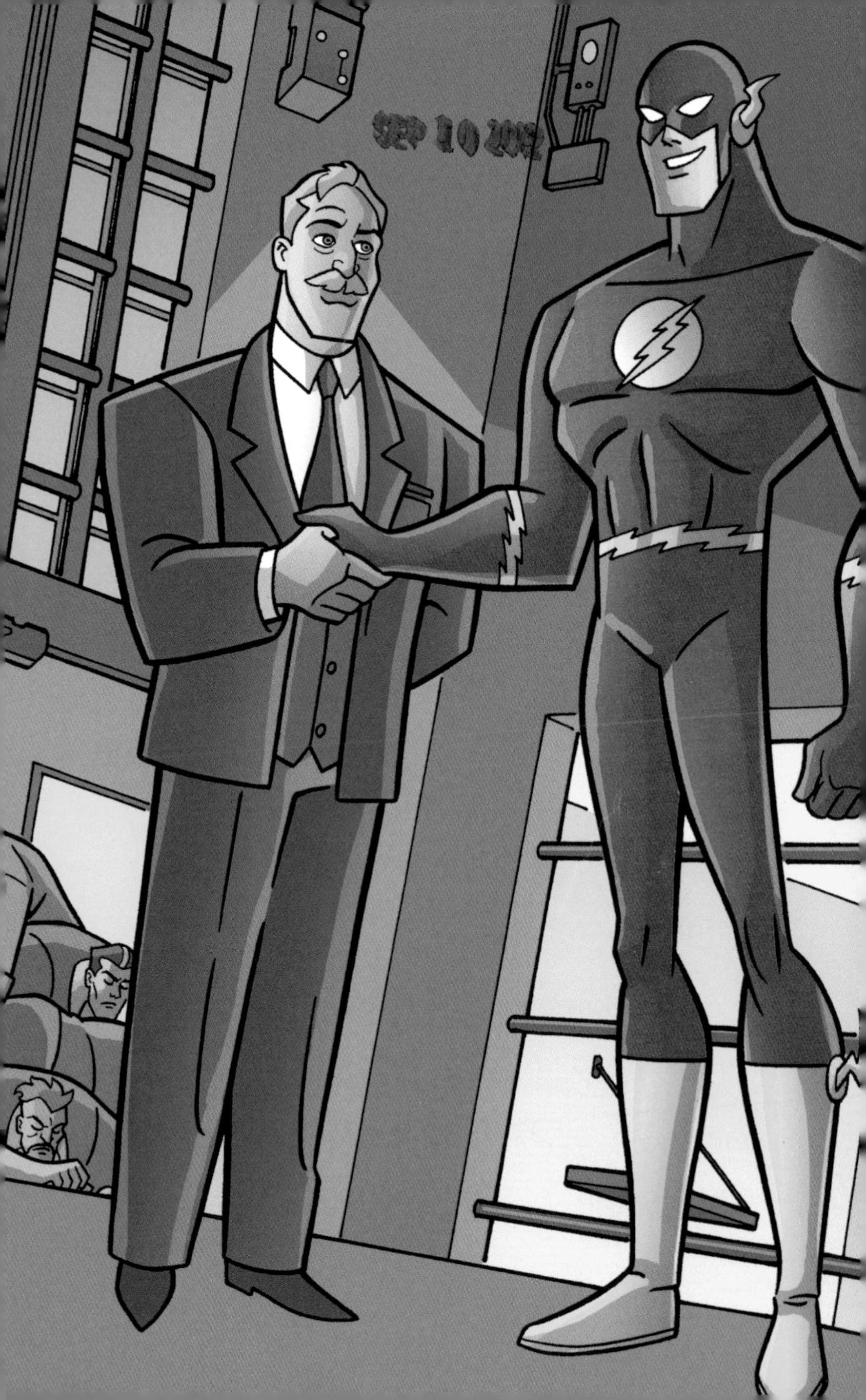

Flash smiled. "Just doing my job," he said. "Think you can handle things from here?"

The warden looked at the pile of groaning criminals at his feet. "Shouldn't be a problem," he said, smirking.

At super-speed, Flash raced around the New Zealand time zone and righted the wrongs that the Clock King had caused. He broke up fights, moved wrecked vehicles out of jammed intersections, and delivered citizens in danger to safety. However, nearly all time-based technology was still malfunctioning.

At least everyone's safe now, he thought. *But I need to find the Clock King.*

CHAPTER 2

MORE BAD NEWS

Clock King watched the news reports of the chaos occurring in New Zealand. The mayhem was all his doing, and he was proud of that fact. He rested his hand on the device next to him, patting it like a puppy dog. "It appears my Time Bomb works splendidly," he said.

Just then, the newscaster paused. An intern whispered into his ear. "Pardon the interruption, viewers," he began, "but we've just received word that the Flash has put a stop to the prison riot in New Zealand!"

"The Flash?" Clock King echoed. "Let's see how he handles more bad news —"

Clock King pushed the *BROADCAST* button on his high-tech computer. Once again, he owned the airwaves.

"I understand that Central City's protector has taken it upon himself to right the wrongs in New Zealand," Clock King said, his cold voice echoing in TV sets across the world. "You may be the Fastest Man Alive, but you'll never catch me."

CLICK! CLICK! He busied himself with the dials and buttons on his Time Bomb. "Next stop — the former Soviet Union!"

BUZZ! The news station returned to its regular broadcast. The host was speechless.

*　　*　　*

Flash had been watching the Clock King's broadcast on a set of TVs from outside a storefront in Wellington, New Zealand. "Well, at least I know where he's heading next."

ZOOOM! Flash took off. As he ran, his eyes narrowed as he thought about the clues Clock King's broadcast had given him. *The Clock King said, "Next stop — the former Soviet Union,"* Flash thought. *That tells me two things: the Clock King has been moving from time zone to time zone along with his Time Bomb, and now he's headed to Russia.*

Flash got to Russia in no time. He knew that only a portion of Eastern Russia lay within the next time zone. *But where will I be needed most?* he wondered.

Suddenly, Flash heard a siren.

Flash followed the siren until he arrived at the source of the sound. To his horror, he now stood outside a nuclear power plant in northeast Russia.

ZWWWOOOOMMMM! He dashed to the control room. A panicked man screamed in surprise as the Flash appeared. But once he realized it was the Scarlet Speedster, the man breathed a sigh of relief.

Flash spoke as slowly as he could, hoping the man could understand him. "How. Can. I. Help?" Flash asked.

The man pointed at the nearby computer screens. Garbled numbers ran across the displays. *Well, that doesn't help,* Flash thought.

Flash shrugged his shoulders as if to say, "I don't understand."

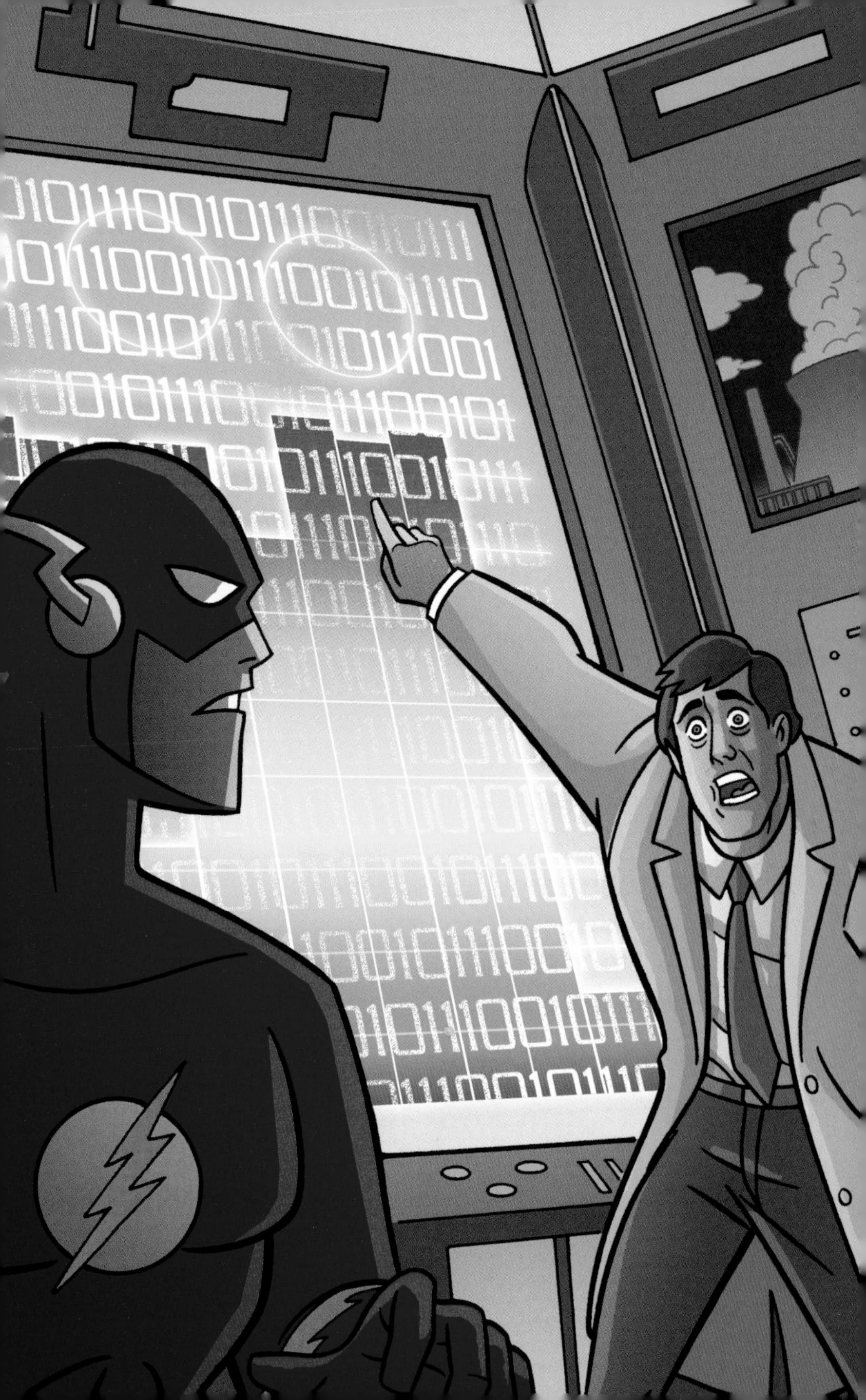

The man blinked and looked down at his feet as if he were thinking. Then, he pointed at the window on the side of the control room.

Flash's eyes went wide. The nuclear core was about to go critical! He had no time to waste. **WHOOOOSH!** Flash stood in front of the door to the nuclear reactor. As he glanced inside, he saw waves of intense heat rippling the air around the core.

Flash pressed the *OPEN* switch next to the door — but it didn't work. Instead, a harsh, metallic **SQUAWK!** burst through the intercom along with a spray of sparks. It made the super hero jump back in shock.

Flash sighed. *Stupid button,* he thought. **WHIR-WHIR-WHIR-WHIR!** Flash vibrated the molecules throughout his entire body.

He had learned to use this skill to match the frequency of solid objects. By vibrating, he was able to pass right through objects.

FLASH! Flash walked through the door. Inside, the heat was overpowering. He could barely breathe. *I better act fast!*

Flash raised his arms toward the reactor and began to spin them in a circle. **WHOOOOSH! WHOOOOSH!** He spun his arms faster and faster until they created two whirlwinds. **THWOOOOMMMMM!!** The cyclones wrapped themselves around the reactor.

In a few moments, the intensely cold air created by his super-speedy arms began to cool the reactor. Flash pumped his arms harder, knowing time was running out.

After a minute, Flash stopped. He placed the palm of his hand on the reactor.

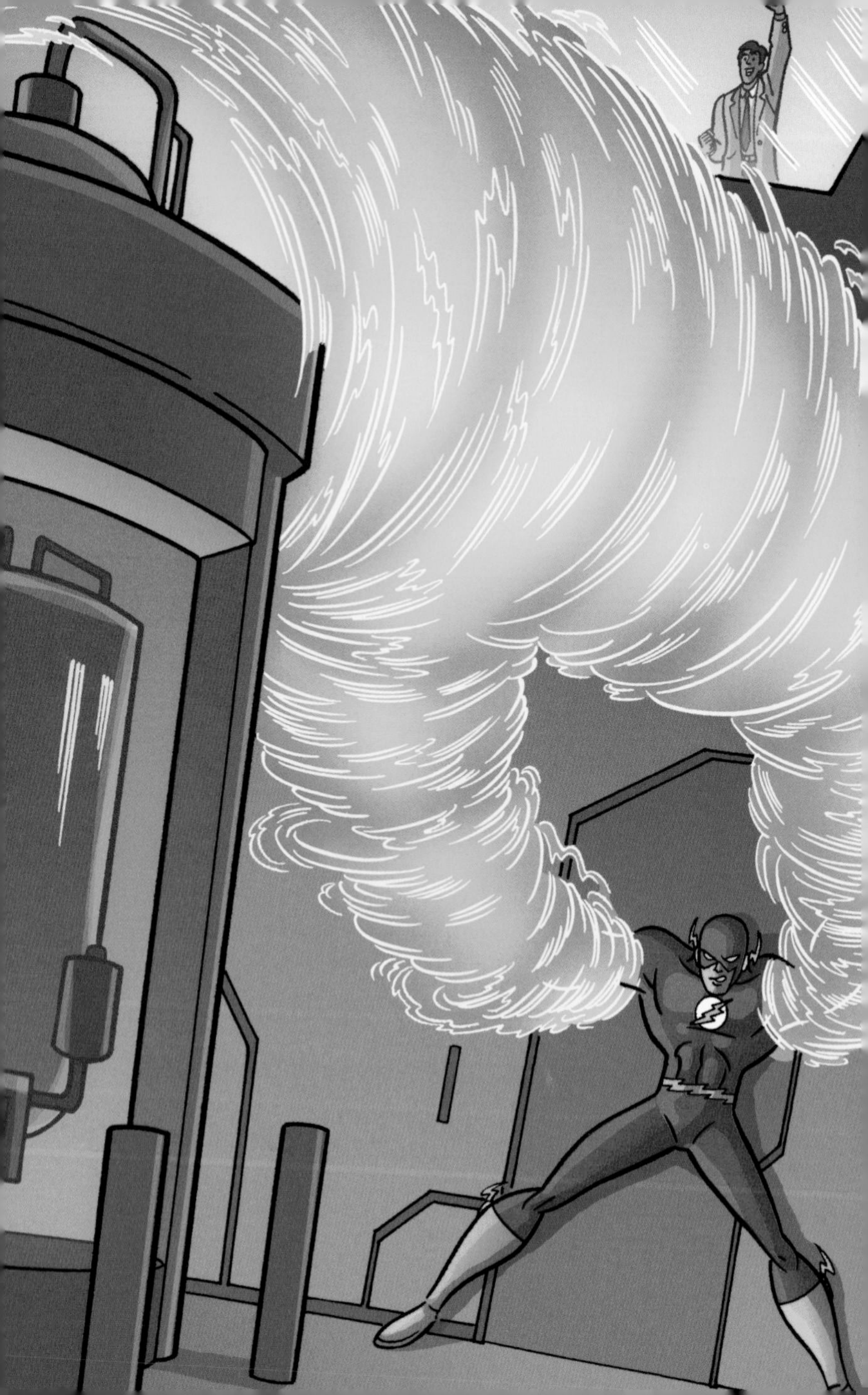

It was cool to the touch. Right on cue, the sirens stopped blasting. "Phew!" Flash said to himself. "That was a close one."

Flash dashed up to the control room. The man who had helped him was cheering.

Flash smiled. *ZOOOM!* He quickly fixed the remaining problems in that time zone. Afterward, he went to each power plant in Russia and warned them to shut down before midnight. This took a long time, but it would make his job much easier when midnight struck in the other time zones.

Flash was weary from the constant action. His muscles ached, his bones hurt, and it felt like it had been days since he last slept. He wanted to rest, but Flash knew that Australian cities in the next time zone would soon need his help.

CHAPTER 3

RUNAWAY TRAIN

Flash came to a stop in Australia. He stood atop Sydney Tower and waited anxiously for midnight — and disaster — to strike . . .

SKREEEEEEECH! Flash didn't have to wait long. Racing far too fast down the street below was the light rail transit — with its brakes still on! It screeched past, sending sparks flying everywhere.

Flash dashed down the side of the building, and then he sprinted alongside the train car.

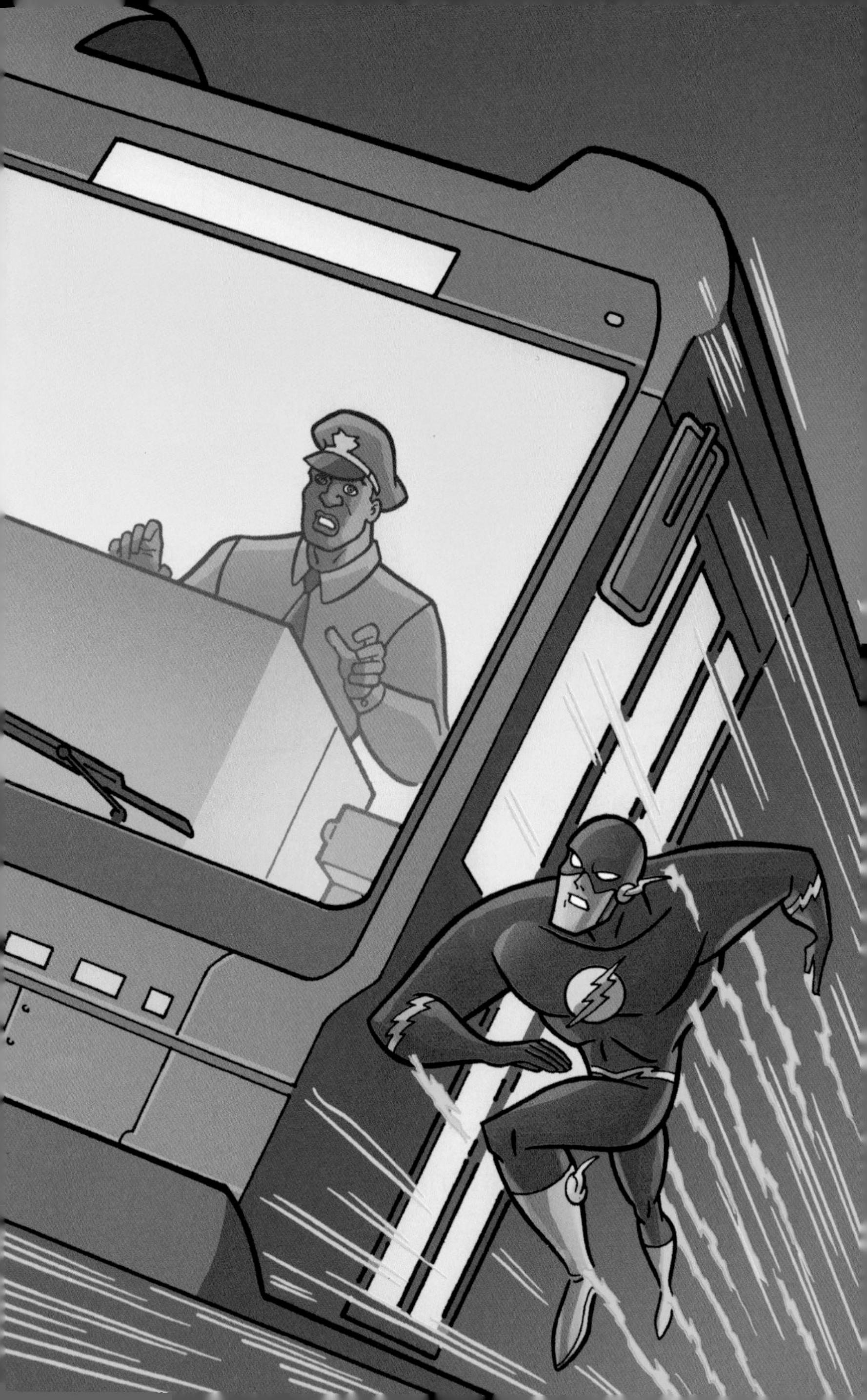

Inside, the conductor appeared to be in shock as the runaway train barreled down the street.

Flash dashed inside and tapped the conductor on his shoulder. **TAP! TAP!**

"Are you okay?" Flash asked, concerned.

The conductor didn't move a muscle. He just continued to stare ahead, wide-eyed and blank-faced.

"Uh-oh," Flash said. He glanced across the panel of seemingly endless buttons, knobs, and switches. "What do all these things do?"

Flash slid a knob all the way to the right. The radio came on. Annoying elevator music filled the cabin.

CLICK! Flash tried another button — but the train just sped up!

Flash sighed. *I have no idea what I'm doing.* He glanced around the cabin and noticed an instruction manual hanging on the wall. *That should help!*

Flash grabbed the conductor's guide and paged through it at super-speed. Halfway down page 142, the text stated that there was a fail-safe switch at every light rail station. The device was mechanical, not electronic, so Flash figured it was likely to bring the train to a halt despite the effects of the Clock King's Time Bomb.

Flash raced outside, down the city street, and up into the nearby railway station. Inside, he scanned the control room and saw the words *FAIL-SAFE SWITCH* written next to a button. He pushed it.

CLICK! Once again, awful elevator music echoed through the station.

"What the heck!" Flash said out loud, grating his teeth. "It says *FAIL-SAFE SWITCH* right next to the button!"

As Flash glanced to his left, he saw a second, bigger button next to the red one he had just pressed. Flash groaned as he realized that the *FAIL-SAFE SWITCH* label was referring to that button, not the one he had just clicked.

I'm so sick of buttons, Flash thought.

Flash pushed the correct button. A loud **BEEP!** rang through the station. A moment later, the rail car pulled into the station and slowed to a screeching halt.

Flash let out a sigh of relief.

ZOOOM! In a split-second, he was back on Sydney Tower, looking for the next disaster that required his attention.

*   *   *

CLICK! Clock King had been watching the news coverage of the Flash's antics in Russia and Australia.

"It's only a matter of time before he figures out my secret and catches up to me," Clock King said to himself. "I need to slow him down."

The villain opened a briefcase next to him. Inside was a device that looked like a high school photo projector. Clock King smiled.

He picked up a handheld radio and spoke into it. "There's been a slight change of plans," he said. "I've decided to make an appearance at our next destination."

A gruff voice on the radio answered. "Roger that."

CHAPTER 4

TIME TRAP

Barry Allen planned his next move at a cafe in Sydney. He watched news coverage of his heroics as the Flash. He was glad Australia was safe, but just as in New Zealand and Russia, the technology that depended on time was still malfunctioning.

Flash had been so busy fixing the disasters in various time zones that he had almost no time to track down the Clock King himself. *If I don't get my hands on him before Hawaii's New Year,* Flash thought, *the world is doomed . . .*

The TV at the cafe let out a **BZZT!** Once again, the Clock King took over the airwaves. But now, he appeared in a tropical area at night. The moon illuminated him in a ghastly glow.

"I'm sure you've been searching desperately for me, Flash," Clock King said, straightening his tie. "Well, I'm out in the open now. Please do me the honor of meeting me on Okinawa Island."

Clock King glanced at his wristwatch. "Just don't make me wait."

BZZT! The transmission ended. Flash didn't hesitate. **ZOOOM!** In a few moments, he was on Okinawa Island. At blinding speed, Flash frantically searched the island until he found Clock King standing by a stream bathed in moonlight. Flash stopped a few feet behind the Clock King.

Beyond the villain, a personal jet idled its engines near a strip of open land. *So that's how he's been traveling from time zone to time zone!* Flash realized.

"Took you long enough, Flash," Clock King said.

"Sorry I'm late," Flash answered.

"Actually," Clock King said, turning to face the Flash. "You're right on time."

Flash saw that the Clock King held a small device with a red button on it. Before Flash could move, Clock King thumbed the switch. **ZZRRRRTT!** A column of blue light burst upward from the sand underneath the Scarlet Speedster's feet.

Alarmed, Flash tried to sprint toward Clock King.

WHAM! Flash hit an invisible wall.

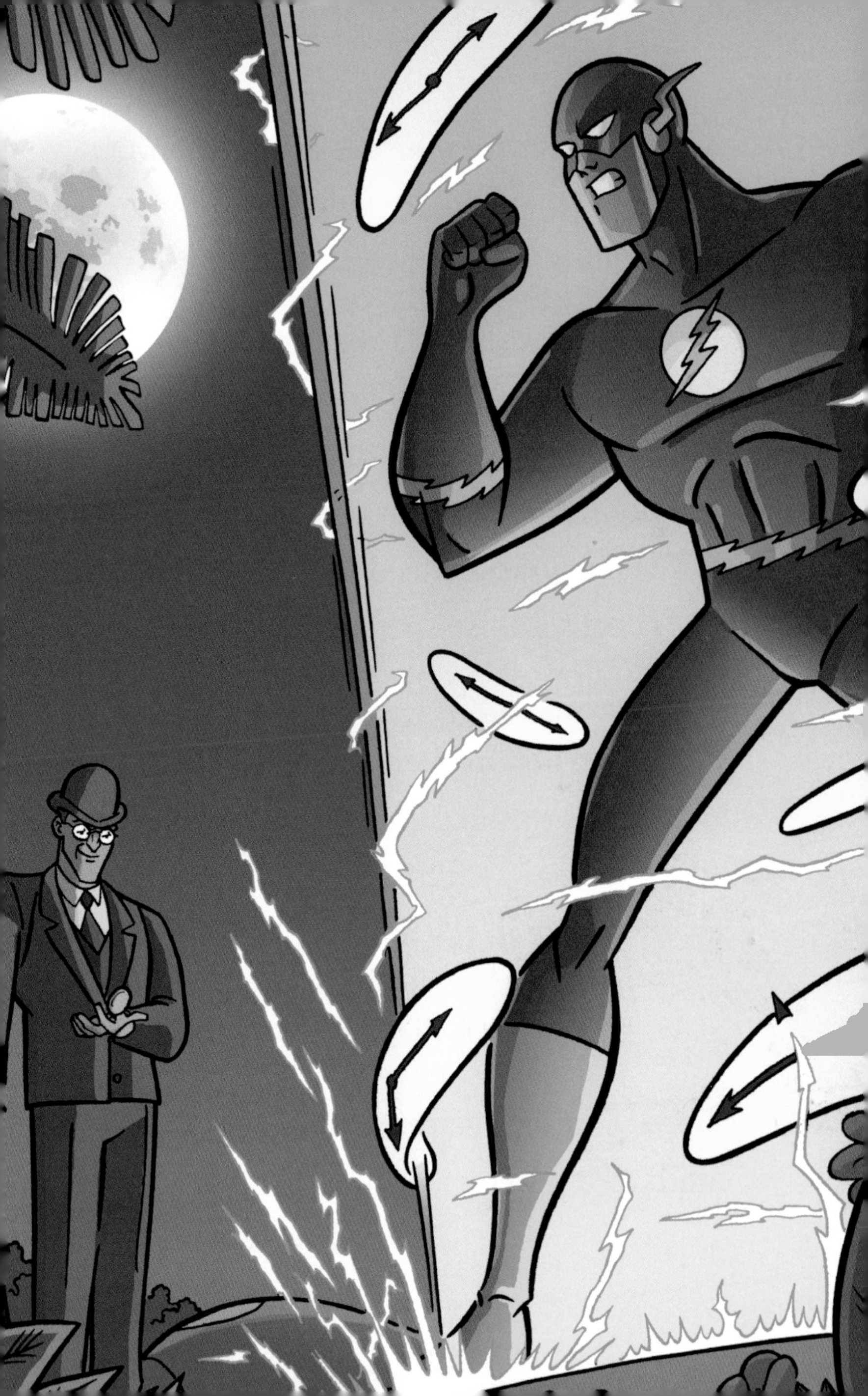

Dazed, Flash reached his hands along the edges of the wall. It circled around him like a human-sized test tube.

Clock King walked toward the Flash and stood nearly face-to-face with the trapped super hero. "I'm afraid there'll be no more running, Flash," Clock King said. "Below your feet is one of my Time Traps. There's no use struggling, as it's quite unbreakable."

Flash watched in silent shock as Clock King gestured at the shore with his open hand. "Nice view, isn't it?" the villain said. "I hope you like it. It's the least I could do, considering you'll be spending the rest of your short life here."

Flash vibrated his molecules as fast as he could and moved forward.

He was trying to pass through the barrier the same way he had passed through the door in the reactor. **THUD!** He smacked into the wall again.

"You see," the villain said, smirking, "the walls of my Time Trap vibrate at nearly the speed of light. No matter how fast you move, you will never be able to vibrate through it and escape."

"I'll find a way out of this, Clock King!" Flash promised.

Clock King smiled. "By the time the sun has risen here, the world will be mine — and you will still be trapped in time."

The villain walked to his airplane and climbed inside. As the pilot began to accelerate across the field, Clock King tipped his hat at the Flash and waved.

*   *   *

As his jet flew closer and closer to the Hawaiian Islands, Clock King patiently counted down the minutes to the last time zone's midnight.

Over the past few hours, Clock King had set off his Time Bomb in several more time zones. Asia, Africa, Antarctica, and the Americas — even the continental United States had all fallen into chaos. Now, only the Hawaiian islands remained unaffected.

As the villain flew toward Hawaii, he knew that the world was nearly his. *In a few minutes, my Time Bomb will be in range of Hawaii,* he thought.

Clock King reclined in his comfortable leather chair and waited.

CHAPTER 5

TURBULENCE

Flash fell to his knees in exhaustion. He had been smashing against the walls of his prison for hours, trying to escape. The full moon was moving farther and farther across the sky. He was nearly out of time.

"There has to be a way out of here," Flash said. The struggle to escape had made him sweat.

As Flash wiped his brow, he noticed that the moonlight illuminated the sweat on his arm. *Wait a second,* Flash thought. *Light is passing through the Time Trap's walls!*

Flash struggled to his feet. *If light can pass through, then there has to be a way that I can, too!* Flash realized.

Flash began to spin in a tight circle. **WHOOOOSH!** His body began to vibrate. He spun faster still. He felt the air around him heat up. He pushed himself harder and faster than ever before. Now, he was vibrating and spinning so fast that he felt the very air around him blend with the molecules in his body.

To an outside observer, the inside of the Time Trap looked like a whirling blur of pure energy. Pure *light*.

Flash could sense that his vibration was nearly in sync with the Time Trap's barrier. **WHIR-WHIR-WHIR-WHIR!** He focused on matching his vibrations with his surroundings.

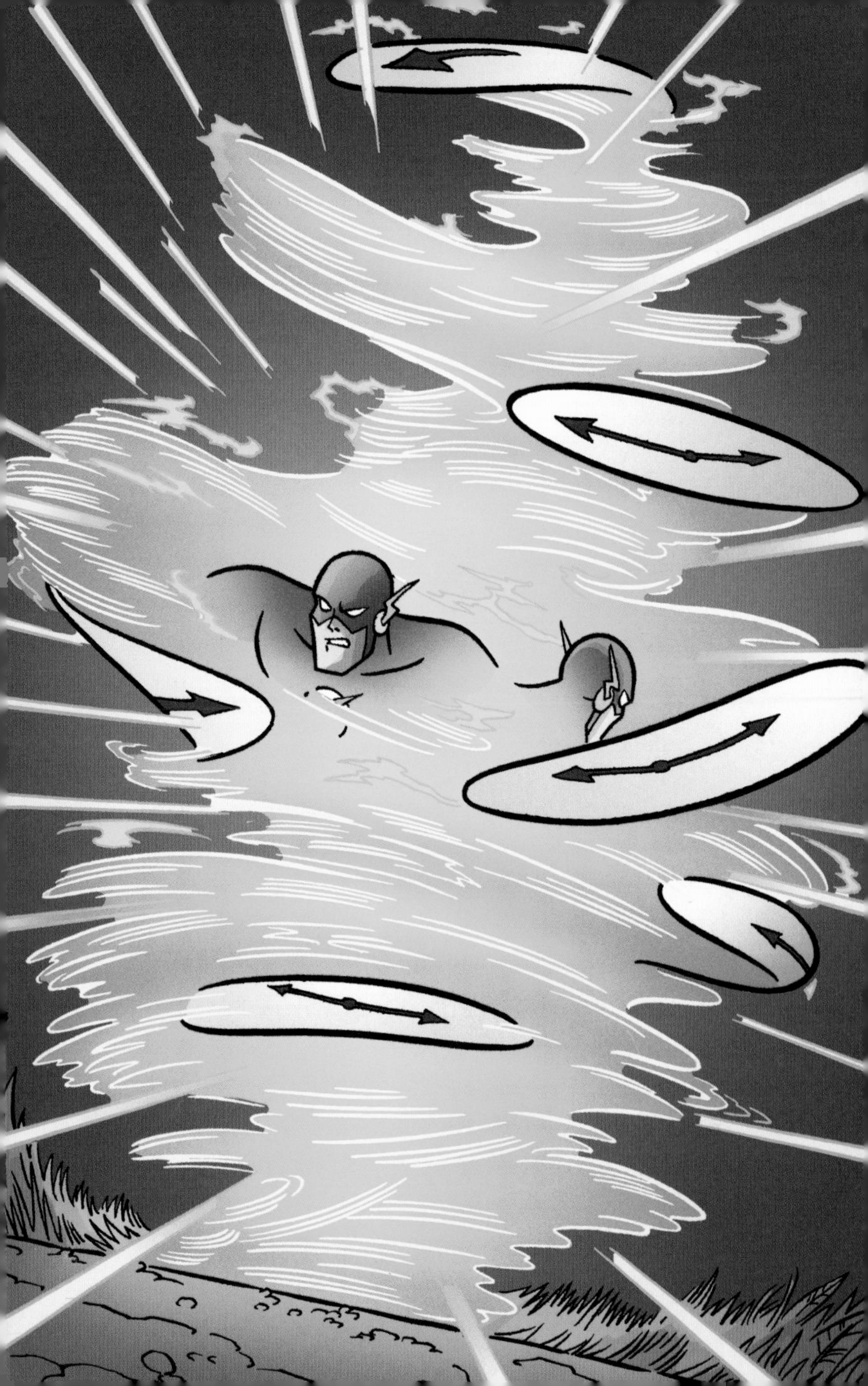

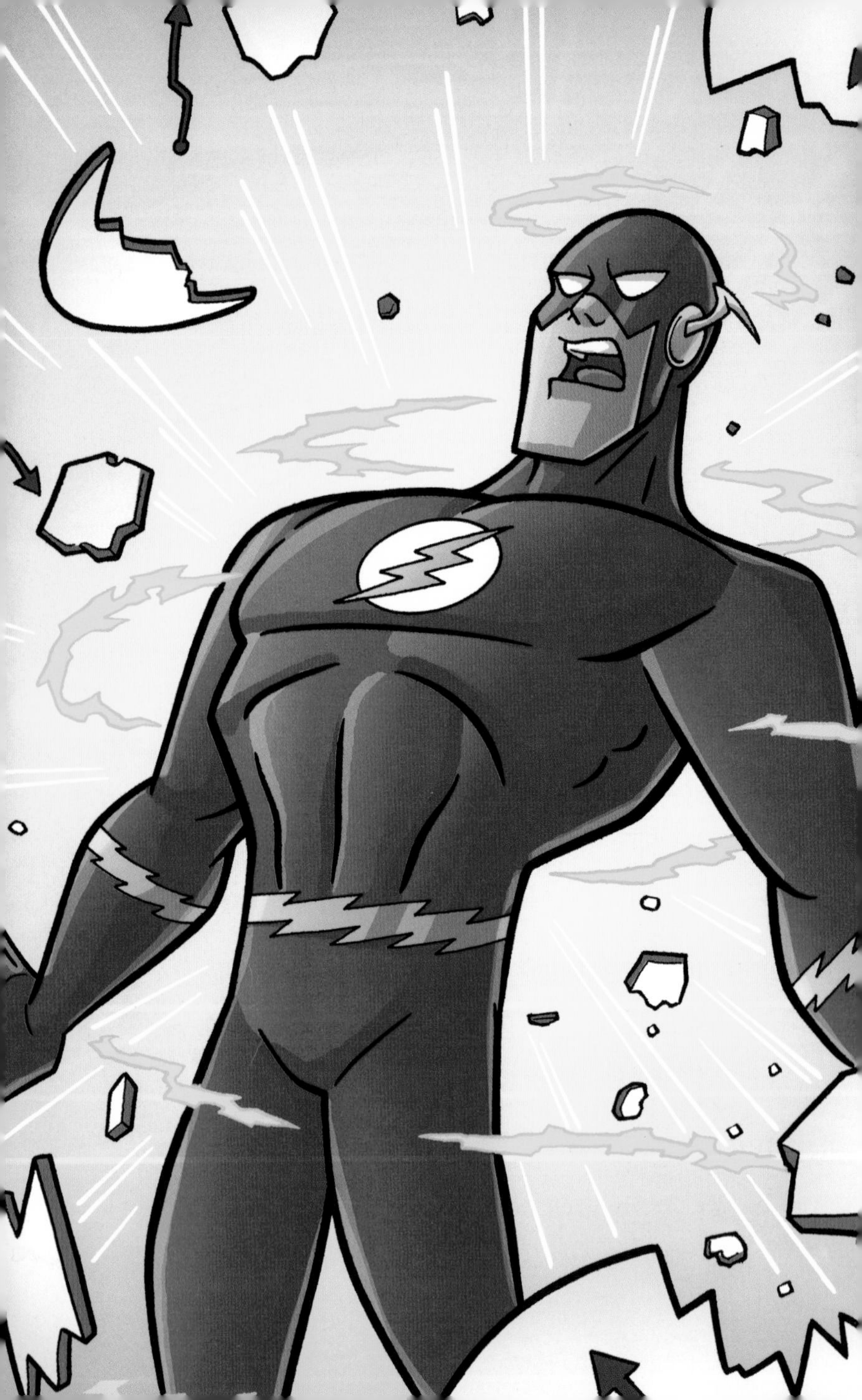

 The walls shattered and Flash was free! He concentrated hard, pulled his molecules back into their normal form, and fell in a heap upon the beach.

Then Flash leaped to his feet and ran across the surface of the ocean at super-speed. *I'm coming for you, Clock King!*

As Flash sprinted across the Pacific Ocean, the moon seemed to be moving backward across the sky. He kept running toward Hawaii.

As he arrived on the island, Flash scanned the skies for any sign of the Clock King. *He'll be flying in from the east,* Flash thought. *I'll head him off there.*

Flash knew Clock King would be flying relatively close to the ground so his Time Bomb would work.

SPLASH! Flash sped out a few miles from the coast and whirled in place, watching and waiting.

Moments later, Flash spotted the plane. Its blinking lights shined brightly in the starry sky. *He probably thinks nothing can stop him now,* Flash thought. *But he's about to hit some serious turbulence . . .*

Flash began to run in a circle atop the water. He spun outward, wider and wider, as he increased his speed. **THWOOOOMMMMM!!** The super-fast motion began to affect the ocean below. It rose upward in a column, twisting and turning like a hurricane!

Flash sent the spinning storm surging upward and into the star-filled sky. Flash carefully timed his movements so that the watery cyclone lined up with the trajectory of the Clock King's airplane.

Flash grinned. *He sure is in for a surprise.*

*   *   *

Clock King relaxed, enjoying the view outside his window. In the distance, he could see the bright city lights of Hilo, Hawaii.

CLICK! He began to adjust dials and buttons on his Time Bomb, preparing to detonate it over the entire Hawaiian time zone. *Just a few more moments,* he thought.

Red lights began flashing inside the cabin. "What is that?!" Clock King said, alarmed. The plane began to shake violently. Objects inside the plane flew across the cabin, crashing into the walls.

Clock King strapped himself into his seat and grabbed his radio. "What's going on?" he yelled at the pilot.

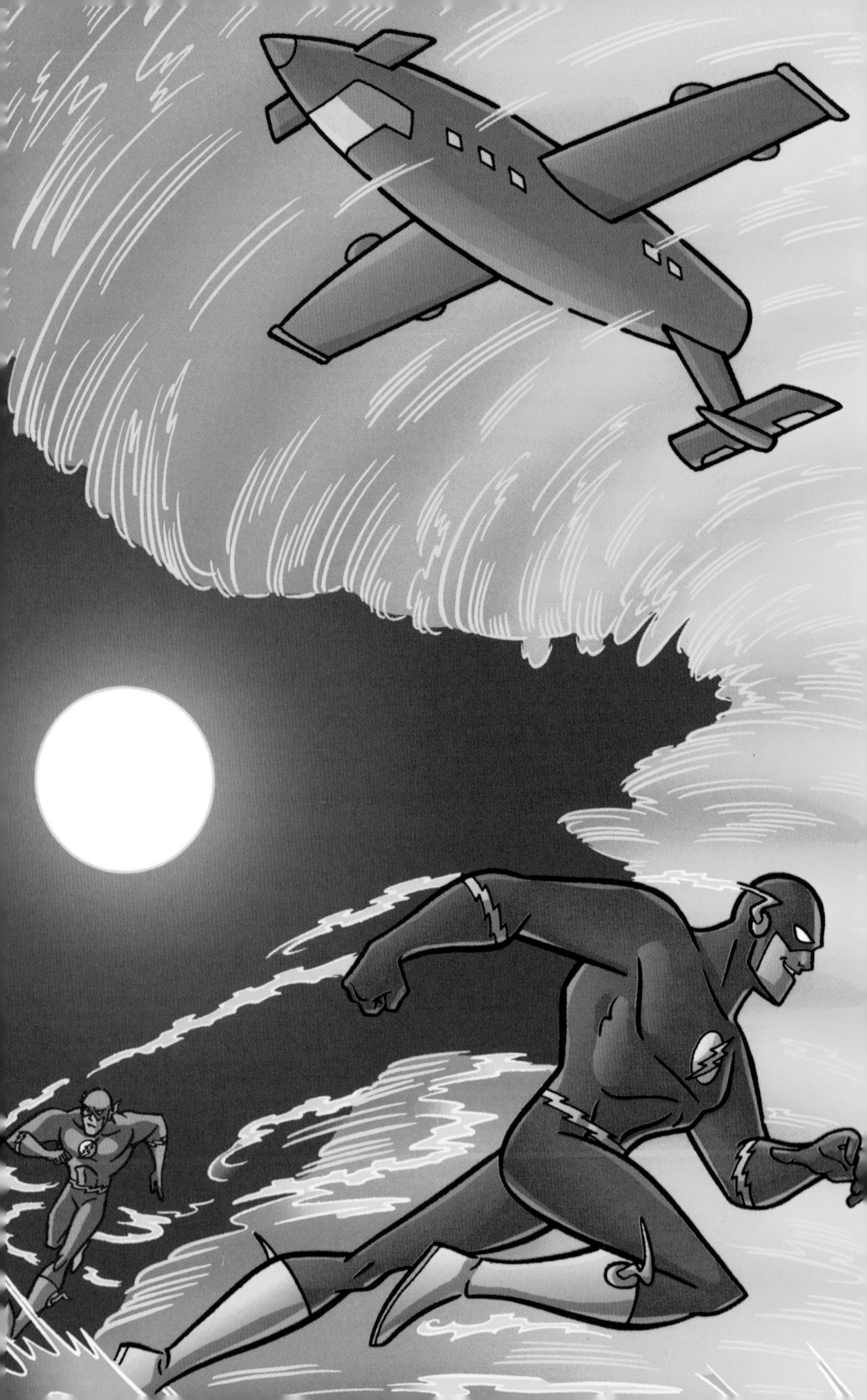

"We've hit some turbulence, sir," the pilot answered.

"But how?" Clock King cried. "The skies are completely clear!"

"I'm not sure, sir, but —" the radio cut out as the plane lurched violently to the side.

"This can't be happening!" The villain howled. He looked out the window to his side. As the plane spun in circles, he saw what looked like a hurricane smashing against the hull of the aircraft! **SLAM!** **THUD!** Both engines cut out.

The plane was now upside down. Everything that wasn't nailed down was resting on the ceiling — including the Time Bomb and the Clock King himself.

Suddenly, the hurricane stopped.

He felt his body push upward, hard against the floor. *We're going down!* Clock King thought, horrified.

The villain closed his eyes. He was sure this was the end for him. *Even if I'm doomed,* he thought. *I can still win.*

The plane hit the water with a  and landed atop the ocean. Clock King was dazed and confused, but he knew he could still activate his Time Bomb. He reached toward it, his finger over the *DETONATE* button.

A burst of intense wind sliced a hole through the plane's hull. Clock King was shocked to see the Flash's smiling face staring down at him!

Flash slapped the villain's hand away from the device at super-speed. Then Flash tossed the villain into his chair and wrapped four seat belts around him. "Sit tight," Flash joked. "I'll be back soon to take you to Iron Heights Penitentiary."

Clock King was not amused. "Another moment, and I would've won," he claimed. "You were very lucky, Flash."

"I wouldn't call it luck," Flash countered. "I'd say it was perfect timing on my part."

The villain stared up at Flash angrily. It was the first time Flash had seen Clock King lose his cool.

Flash walked over to the Time Bomb.

Flash eyed the device. He saw that there were two buttons, marked DETONATE and DEACTIVATE.

I haven't had much luck with buttons today, Flash thought. *But I have a feeling things will be different this time.*

Flash picked up the device and walked toward the hole in the plane. He took a deep breath. Flash would have to visit every time zone and restore order to technology around the world. Fortunately, because of his super-speed, it would only take him a few minutes to right the wrongs that the Clock King had caused.

"This isn't over, Flash," Clock King warned. "I'll bide my time and get my revenge when you least expect it!"

"Maybe," Flash admitted, smirking at the villain. "But from now on, I'll be keeping my eye on the Clock."

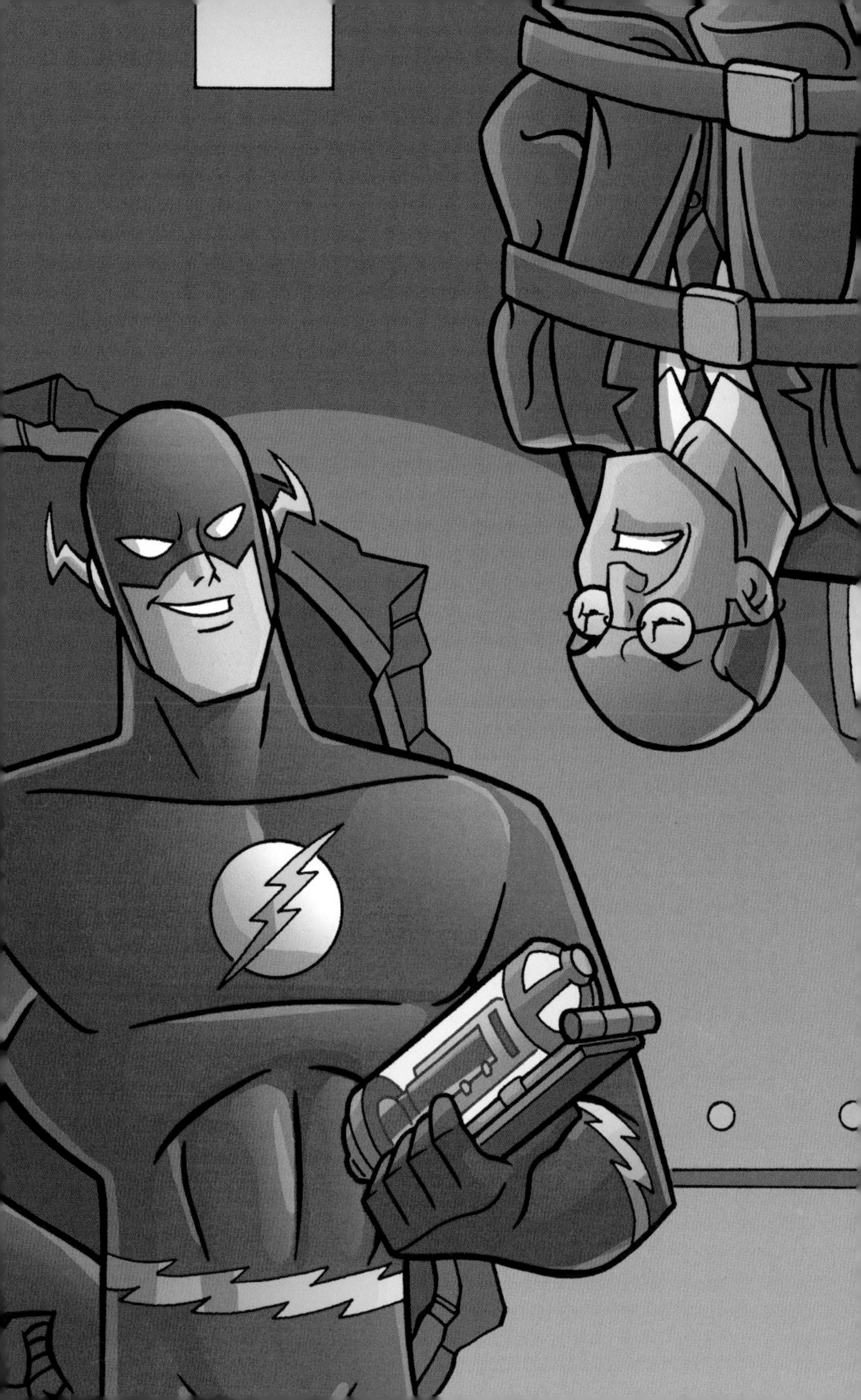

File Edit View Go Window Help

CLOCK KING

THE CLOCK KING

REAL NAME: TEMPLE FUGATE

OCCUPATION: PROFESSIONAL CRIMINAL

HEIGHT: 5' 10"

WEIGHT: 173 LBS.

EYES: BROWN

HAIR: BROWNISH-GRAY

SPECIAL POWERS/ABILITIES:

Innate sense of timing and punctuality; talented and practiced swordsman; technological knowledge; he is also a gifted planner and strategist.

done

CLOCK KING BIO

BIOGRAPHY:

Temple Fugate has a gift for timing and punctuality, which has served him well over the years. Originally, Fugate was an efficiency expert who never missed a beat. Businesses from all over came to him for planning and strategy assistance – until he was late to his job for the first time ever. The misstep cost him dearly – he lost his riches, respect, and his job. Ever since, Fugate has tormented and terrorized anyone who doesn't respect punctuality and time as the cold and calculating super-villain, the Clock King.

CLOCK KING FACTS

Temple Fugate's name is a play on the Latin phrase, *tempus fugit*, which means "time flies."

Fugate has no superpowers, but his sense of timing and fencing skills make him quite deadly.

Clock King has faced off with Batman several times, nearly defeating the Dark Knight twice.

BIOGRAPHIES

Sean Tulien is a children's book editor living and working in Minnesota. In his spare time, he likes to read, eat sushi, play video games, exercise outdoors, concoct evil schemes, listen to loud music, and write books like this one.

Dan Schoening was born in Victoria, B.C. Canada. From an early age, Dan has had a passion for animation and comic books. Currently, Dan does freelance work in the animation and game industry and spends a lot of time with his lovely little daughter, Paige.

GLOSSARY

detonate (DET-uh-nate)—to set off an explosion

device (di-VISSE)—a piece of equipment that does a particular job

digital (DIJ-uh-tuhl)—a digital clock's display shows time in numerals

emerged (i-MURJD)—came into the open

high-tech (HYE TEK)—advanced, as in technology

interference (in-tur-FEER-uhnzs)—the interruption of a signal that prevents technology from working

interrupt (in-tuh-RUHPT)—stop or hinder in the middle of something

malfunction (mal-FUHNGK-shuhn)—to stop working properly

molecules (MOL-uh-kyoolz)—the smallest parts of a subtance that still display all the properties of that substance

vibrate (VYE-brate)—to move back and forth rapidly

DISCUSSION QUESTIONS

1. At what point in the story did you figure out that the Clock King was traveling by airplane? What clue did you pick up on?

2. Which heroic feat that Flash performed in this book was most impressive? Why?

3. This book has ten illustrations. Which one is your favorite? Why?

WRITING PROMPTS

1. Lots of disasters occurred when the Clock King's Time Bomb went off. What are some other problems that could occur if all the world's clocks shut down? Write about it.

2. If you could travel at super-speed like the Flash, what would you do with your superpowers? Write about your experiences as a super hero.

3. Why is time important? How would life be different if we didn't have clocks? Write about a life without clocks.

THE FUN DOESN'T STOP HERE!

DISCOVER MORE AT....
www.CAPSTONEKIDS.COM

GAMES & PUZZLES
VIDEOS & CONTESTS
HEROES & VILLAINS
AUTHORS & ILLUSTRATORS

FIND COOL WEBSITES AND
MORE BOOKS LIKE THIS ONE
AT WWW.FACTHOUND.COM.

JUST TYPE IN THE BOOK ID:
9781434226266
AND YOU'RE READY TO GO!

MORE NEW
The FLASH ADVENTURES!

CAPTAIN BOOMERANG'S
COMEBACK!

MASTER OF MIRRORS!

TRICKSTER'S BUBBLE
TROUBLE

KILLER KALEIDOSCOPE

ICE AND FLAME

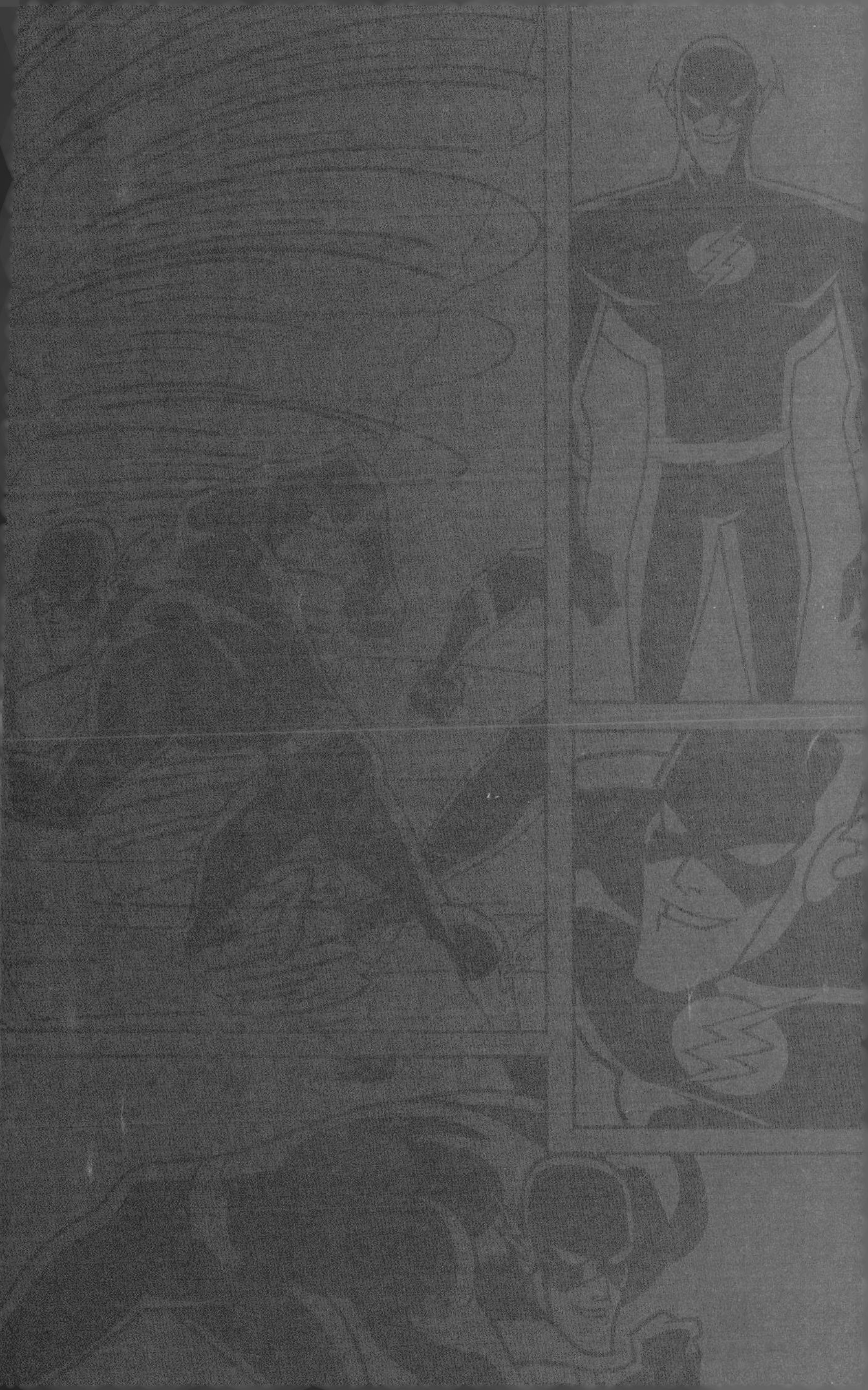

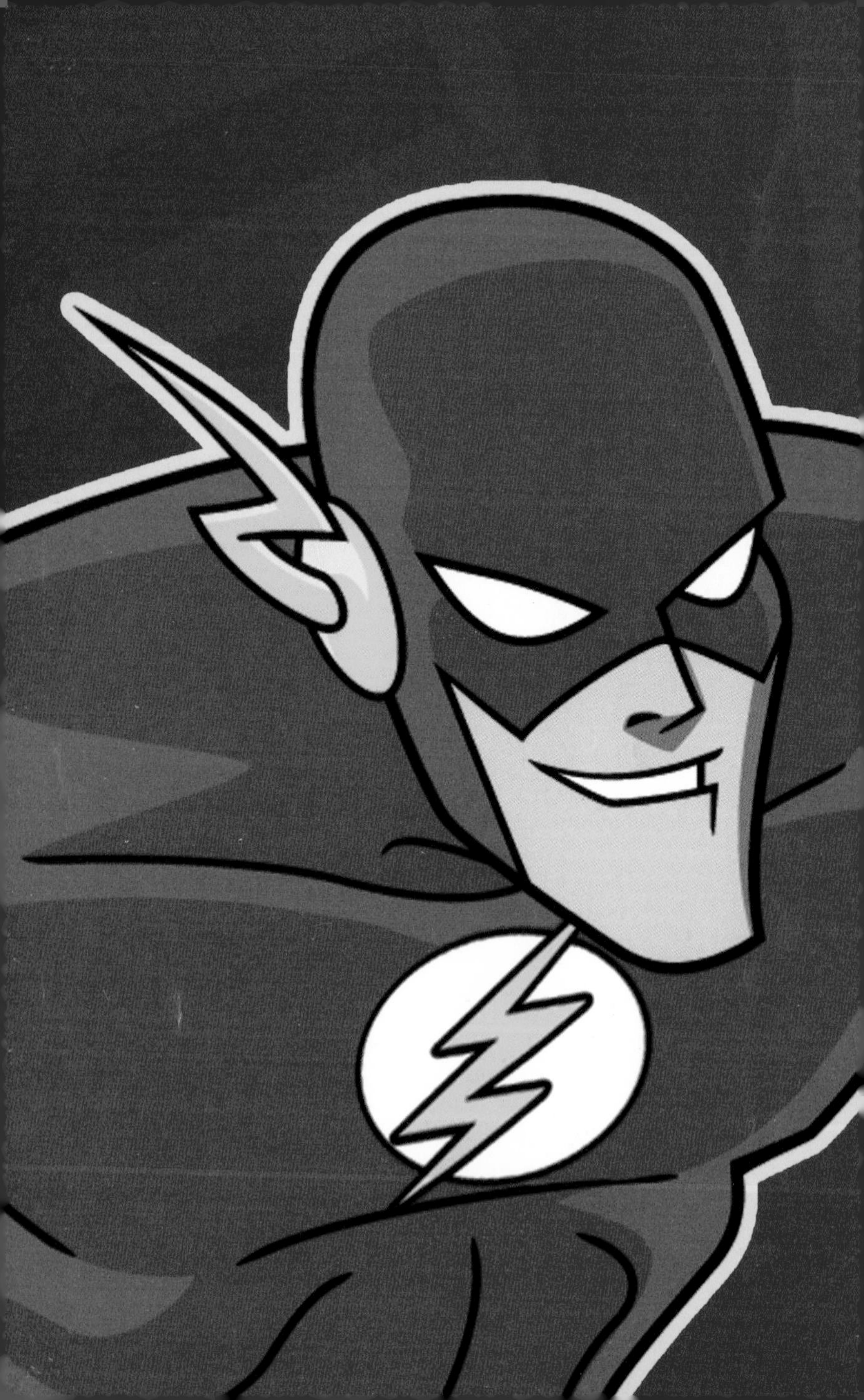